Cinderella

(as if you didn't already know the story)

Cinderella

(as if you didn't already know the story)

by
barbara
ensor

schwartz & wade books · new york

If somebody really does remind me you of someone real, is that a crime against the law?

Copyright © 2006 by Barbara Ensor
Published in the United States by Schwartz & Wade Books, an imprint of Random House Children's Books, a division of Random House, Inc., New York.
Schwartz & Wade Books and colophon are trademarks of Random House, Inc.
www.randomhouse.com/kids
Educators and librarians, for a variety of teaching tools, visit us at
www.randomhouse.com/teachers

Library of Congress Cataloging-in-Publication Data
Ensor, Barbara
Cinderella (as if you didn't already know the story) / by Barbara Ensor.—1st ed.
p. cm.
Summary: In this updated version of the Cinderella story, Cinderella writes letters to her dead mother apologizing for not being more assertive, which she remedies soon after marrying the prince.
ISBN 0-375-83620-9 (trade) – ISBN 0-375-93620-3 (lib. bdg.)
[1. Fairy tales. 2. Folklore.] I. Title: Cinderella (as if you didn't already know the story). II. Cinderella. English. III. Title.
PZ8.E596Ci 2006
[398.2]–dc22
2005012999
Manufactured in China
10 9 8 7 6 5 4 3 2 1
First Edition

ANNE SCHWARTZ AND LEE WADE WAVED MAGIC WANDS TO MAKE THIS BOOK HAPPEN

THANKS TO DOVER PUBLICATIONS FOR PICTURE RESOURCES

SPECIAL THANKS TO JULIETTE BORDA, BRITTANY BURKE, DAVID COWAN, MADELINE CRAVENS, KAROLINA ENSOR, VALORIE FISHER, KAREN HATT, DEXTER HOFFMAN, GEORGIA HOFFMAN, MATT MITLER, BRIDGET ORR, STEVE RICHARDSON & MICHAEL RICHARDSON-WILSON

This story, based on a version of "Cinderella" written by Charles Perrault in 1697

For my father

C inderella is what I am calling her from the beginning, even though I don't know what people actually called her back then. I'm definitely not just going to call her Charlene when for all I know her name was Naomi, because that's how rumors start. Like the one about the stepsisters being ugly, which is such a lie. The truth is, they were nice enough to look at, maybe not as pretty as you or Cinderella, but certainly not ugly. All right, some of what they *said* was ugly, yes, I agree, but we are getting ahead of ourselves now. Trust me, everything else in this story is one hundred percent true.

Cinderella was a little older than you when this whole thing started, a really nice girl. I'm sure the two of you would have liked each other. (Too bad you didn't know her then; Cinderella could so have used a friend like you.)

Now the actual story is about to begin.

chapter 1

"If anyone knows of any reason why this couple should not be joined in holy matrimony, let them speak now or forever hold their peace."

Nobody said anything out loud during the brief silence that hung over the room after the minister spoke those words. So the wedding ceremony for Cinderella's father and her new stepmother went ahead as planned. (In case you want to know if the children of one person not liking the children of the person they are marrying would be enough reason to call a wedding off, the answer is NO. Because in a strict legal sense only the adults are getting married.) Nothing else could be said or done after the minister told everyone the couple was now

"man   and   wife."

Nice for *her,* Cinderella thought, but my dad was *already* a man.

Still, if this made her dad happy, it made Cinderella happy too. And all the guests thought she should be happy.

"You lucky girl!"

"I bet you're thrilled!"

Of course she was, and she was smiling at everyone so that there would be no doubt about it.

Cinderella did feel a little queasy, though. She hadn't been able to get to sleep the night before, and it didn't help that her real mother wasn't around to smooth the sheets and give her a cup of warm milk. Cinderella didn't love her stepmother yet, and she didn't love her new stepsisters either . . . but she decided that was perfectly okay.

"First you have to get to know them" was what her mother would have said, and it was true. What was also true, though, was that Cinderella didn't even think she *liked* them. A person couldn't help noticing,

they didn't seem very friendly.

It made the edges of her smile hard to hold up.

Cinderella's mother was no longer alive. But for some reason Cinderella couldn't help worrying about what it would be like if her mother ran into the new stepmother as they were both heading to the bathroom in the middle of the night. Or if the two of them were trying to make coffee at the same time. It wouldn't be pretty.

⚫

After the ceremony Cinderella went back to her room, took off her stiff patent leather shoes,

and began to write.

Dear Mama,

I regret to inform you that ~~Dad~~ your husband has married ~~again~~ a second time. ~~This is perfectly legal. It did seem a little soon.~~ I don't expect you will be able to read this, but in case you can I did want to be the one to tell you myself. ~~so you don't find out about it in an unpleasant way.~~

The lady has two daughters
who are older than me. To be
honest, and don't repeat this to
anyone, they seem a little stuck-up.
I'm sure everything will work out
fine—Dad says it will. I hope
this isn't too much of a shock. ~~It's~~
~~not going to be a real family like you and~~
~~me and Dad~~. They are moving a bunch
of furniture pretty soon, so I gotta go.
Your Daughter
4 ever,

Cupcake

· 13 ·

P.S. Does everyone always
talk about how the bride looks?
Do they mean she looks good
in comparison to how she looks
on other days? I don't get it. I
guess I'll have to figure it out
on my own.

P.P.S.

Don't worry about
writing back,
I don't expect miracles
or anything.
(we don't believe in them,)
or do we?

chapter 2

The honey-colored wallpaper, candy pink curtains, and comfy furniture that Cinderella and her mother had picked out so carefully all made her stepmother shudder.

"So sweet!" her stepmother said, and managed to make it sound like an insult. Then she went out and hired a professional decorator to help her express what she called her "personal vision for the interior." Every picture of Cinderella's mother—except "Well, all right, just that one over the kitchen mantel"—had to go. And it wasn't "Dad's room" anymore; it was suddenly "our room." Already it smelled of her step-mother's icky perfume. Cinderella felt sorry for the house itself, which had a sadness about it now, like a tugboat forced to dress up as a yacht.

If you had visited Cinderella's house

a week after the wedding, you would hardly have recognized it. Sprawled on a four-poster bed, in what used to be Cinderella's room, her elder stepsister was complaining about "what a dump" they had moved into. Next door the second stepsister was telling a friend what a "weirdo" their new sibling was. On her way to her own room, Cinderella always tiptoed by their doors to give the girls a little privacy.

Cinderella's new room was at the very top of the house—where it got roasting hot in the summertime and you had to huddle under lots of blankets in the wintertime. The only place she could stand up straight was in the very center.

"My girls' furniture could not possibly fit up there," her stepmother had explained with a helpless little shrug.

Dear Mama,
As you might have
noticed, I am sleeping in
the attic now, where you
didn't even think we should
put the kittens! I have
to admit I didn't say anything,
but don't get mad. I knew
my stepsisters would get the
good rooms anyway, and they
would turn all — red in
the face if I showed I minded.
I thought maybe they would

begin to ~~love~~ like
me if I just moved
my stuff without
complaining.

Unfortunately,
that didn't exactly
work. If you were
here I ~~wou~~ bet you could
help me stand up to my new

Stepmother. But of course if you were here, I wouldn't need to (not that it's your fault or anything). I miss you a lot.

Bye 4 now,
Cupcake

P.S. Dad looks a little pale. He might be working too hard.

Cinderella didn't see much of her father anymore. When he was around he always seemed to be in a hurry to get to the office. He was an accountant. Now that he had married Cinderella's stepmother, he had decided to stop playing clarinet with the bebop band on Tuesday nights.

"I can't believe what you spent on that woman's funeral!" Cinderella's stepmother would often say as her father slipped out the back door in the morning. Cinderella was usually asleep when he got home, tired out from all her chores.

And there were always lots of chores. A long list would be waiting for Cinderella when she got home from school.

1. Sweep the stairs

2. Don't answer the door in your work clothes

3. Get rid of fingerprints on the light switches

4. Look a little cheerful

5. Do not hum

6. Clean the toilets

7. Don't complain to your father

8. Crumbs in the kitchen encourage mice, so clean up *immediately* after your sisters

It all had to be finished before Cinderella went to bed. If her stepmother didn't like the way something was done, she would throw a conniption fit.

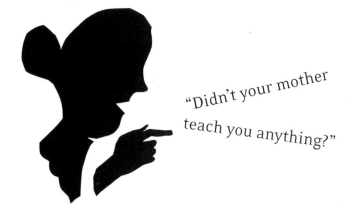

"Didn't your mother teach you anything?"

Sometimes it seemed as though the more Cinderella tried to make her stepmother happy, the more angry her stepmother became. When that happened, Cinderella would imagine the skin on her face stretched out flat—like a balloon that was too full of air. This made it easier for Cinderella to look like she was paying attention when her stepmother spoke, without being stung by her cruel words.

chapter 3

After mopping the floor one Saturday morning, Cinderella settled onto the wooden chair by the fireplace. From where she sat, she and her mother's picture could see each other pretty well. Cinderella was just about to tell her mom about the tomatoes that were almost ready to pick in her vegetable garden when her stepsisters burst noisily into the room. Cinderella could tell they were in one of their giddy giggly moods.

(Now, remember, I told you before, nobody called her Cinderella yet.)

Just the sight of their earnest little stepsister, wearing dirty hand-me-downs and gazing at the burnt-out cinders from last night's fire, struck the two of them as hilariously funny. "Cin-der-ella!" the elder one said in a low singsong voice, and they both howled with laughter.

Soon it was

"Cinderella, have you cleaned my room yet?"

"Cinderella, my shoes need to be sorted by color."

And even her stepmother would call
out,

"Cinderella,
my dress needs
ironing—right now!"

or

"Cinderella, there's a dead mouse in my room!"

Cinderella was her name.

The poor girl seemed to be running up and down stairs all the time now. To the basement for a pair of gloves, to the attic to get the ironing board, to the kitchen to make a face pack, then up the stairs to the bathroom to start in with the curling iron. She couldn't seem to run fast enough. She would have done anything to make them like her—even just a tiny little bit—but nothing worked.

"What is *wrong* with you?"

Her stepsisters were impossible to please.

"So are you coming to the ball or what?" the elder stepsister asked Cinderella one day. Two pairs of eyes neatly outlined with eyeliner (with powdered lids and lashes loaded with mascara) looked intently at Cinderella.

"Ball?" asked Cinderella, taken aback.

"I didn't know there was going to be a ball."

"She thinks we like trying out new hairstyles every day of the week," the younger one giggled, nudging her sister.

"All three of us have been invited to

the prince's ball," the elder explained slowly, as if English were not Cinderella's native tongue.

"It's at the palace," the second stepsister added, patiently. "Everyone's going to be there. I mean, you know, not *everyone,* but . . ."

"Technically, you see," the elder continued, "the invitation is for you as well."

"Strictly speaking," added the younger one, to underline the theoretical nature of Cinderella's invitation.

It was not hard to see what her step-sisters wanted her to say.

Cinderella swallowed hard. "I think . . . I'd better not," she said.

"Got something more important going on that evening?" inquired the elder, catching her sister's eye.

"I don't have the right clothes, and it would be too . . . weird," said Cinderella quickly, looking away, in case her eyes began to tear up.

"Suit yourself," her stepsisters said.

Obviously relieved, the two of them began clawing through rings and bracelets in their jewelry boxes.

The next morning, Cinderella wrote to her mother.

Dear Mama,

~~Please~~ Don't be mad at me. I know you are already. What fun would it be going to the ball with everyone wishing I wasn't there?

She tore the letter into tiny pieces without writing any more. She didn't like the feeling that her mom was looking over her shoulder disagreeing with every word she wrote.

The ball would be that very evening.

As her stepsisters surveyed themselves in the full-length mirror, Cinderella wound strands of their hair around a curling iron to make ringlets.

"Maybe the prince will pick one of you two for his bride—I would if I were he!" their mother said, poking her head around the door. "Then we could all get out of here and go live in the palace."

As she looked more closely, she spotted a speck of lint on the younger daughter's gown and angrily went to pick it off.

"If he doesn't marry one of you, we will all know who to blame!"

Dear Mama,
This might not interest you all that much, but I did want to stay in touch.

Here are some sketches of the dresses my stepsisters have pretty much decided to wear. I really hope they don't change their minds again. (Because I'd never be able to finish fixing up new ones in time and they'd get so mad.)

Anyway, I've got
to sew on
some
buttons,
better run.

Hope you are well, Cupcake

It's kind of hard to
get their hair
to stay up
like this.

chapter 4

"I bet our little stepsister wishes she were coming now," the younger sister said as she took a last look at herself in the mirror.

"Too late!" said the elder one triumphantly.

"You both look gorgeous. Have a wonderful time."

Cinderella closed the door and sat down next to a pile of laundry to have a good cry.

"You wish you could go to the ball, don't you?" said a total stranger who was suddenly standing next to her.

Cinderella, too shocked to say anything, nodded mutely.

"I'm your fairy god-mother," the lady said, as though this would clear up any confusion.

Cinderella could not wipe the startled look off her face.

"I don't know why you look so surprised," said her

godmother, starting to sound impatient.

Cinderella opened and closed her mouth a few times, but no words came out.

"We'll have you on your way in no time, Cupcake," her godmother continued breezily. "There are a few little errands your godmother needs you to help her with first. Could you get me that rather nice pumpkin I noticed out in the garden?"

After that the fairy's demands became more challenging. "Your mother used to have one of those thingamajigs," her godmother announced, pantomiming that she was a prisoner behind bars.

"Huh?" replied Cinderella.

"You know, for catching mice!"

Cinderella ran two steps at a time

down to the basement. Six mice had followed the smell of cheese into the trap.
Now they were waiting to be let loose in
the garden again, as per usual.

"Perfect!"

said her godmother when the metal box

full of rodents was set down in front of her.

"Now I need a really top-notch driver," she said, and she cast her eyes around the room. "Someone really trustworthy, who has a way with the horses."

"I'll check the rat trap," said Cinderella, surprised to hear the words coming out of her mouth.

"Terrific idea!" said her godmother, her eyes lighting up.

Cinderella came back with a particularly hideous fat old rat, which clearly delighted the fairy.

"Now stand back," she said importantly. A wave of her wand transformed the whiskered rat into a nattily attired driver for the coach. His whiskers became a mustache, carefully waxed to curve up like the handlebars on a bicycle. His pointy nose poked out eagerly from under a top hat. His girth took on an air of distinction beneath an expertly tailored suit. Already the former rat was enthusiastically cracking a whip.

"Do hold your horses, Charles!" Cinderella's godmother scolded him gently. There were no horses yet, and Charles the coachman looked suitably embarrassed.

Like a child joyfully waving a sparkler, the fairy godmother crisscrossed her wand, and the sturdy orange pumpkin exploded into an elegant gold coach supported by delicate wheels. The sumptuous interior was upholstered in a tartan plaid. A gentle tap on the head of each gray mouse produced a group of startled horses. The coachman patted each of the dappled team in a way that settled them down immediately. They were ready to go anywhere.

Cinderella could not believe her fairy godmother was going to all this trouble for her. She was about to tell her it wasn't necessary when her godmother barked another order. "Be a good girl and get me, um . . ."

She bit her lip, looking to see what was missing. "Some nice-looking lizards, I saw some in your garden. . . ."

While her godmother was still trying to remember exactly where it was she had seen them . . . six lizards that had been sunning themselves on a flat rock were abruptly awakened. Cinderella reached for them one by one. With their tails clasped gently between her thumb and forefinger, she presented them to her fairy godmother.

"Oh yessss!" said the godmother, delighted with the wriggly mass. A rhythmic motion of the wand turned them into six silk-clad coachmen chatting about last night's football game. The former lizards clung effortlessly to the decorative doodads all over the coach.

"And now it's your turn, my dear. My goodness, you are as lovely as your mother." Her godmother's wand traced

circles around Cinderella, who in-
stantly began to change.

chapter 5

There was a whooshing sound, then a pop like a cork being pulled out of a champagne bottle, and then Cinderella let out a little scream. The person in the mirror hardly even looked familiar. Some spark of beauty, scarcely visible to the naked eye before, had become a blazing fire. A new dress, simple, floaty, and elegant, was almost part of her. Gorgeous ivory-colored shoes with curlicued gold trim peeked out below her petticoat. Peering closely into the mirror, Cinderella checked to see if it was really her.

Yes, the legs in sheer stockings had kicked soccer balls into goals, pedaled tricycles, and knelt to sweep ashes from the fireplace. The heart beating in her chest was the same heart that loved her mother. The face in the mirror, her face, was flushed with excitement. Cinderella gave herself a little hug.

Her fairy godmother told the driver not to go too fast. Then, turning to Cinderella, she said sternly, "You need to be home by midnight, dear. That's part of the package. *Midnight,* do you hear me?

"And by the way, dear, do you like the shoes?"

Cinderella nodded that she did. She was still trying to take it all in. She had woken up a girl that morning. Now she was something else, a butterfly released from its chrysalis. For a moment, she thought about running back

to her room and locking the door. She wanted to get under the blankets and write a letter to her mother.

Then she took a deep breath. She saw

that the driver and horses were restless to trot into the night air. Cinderella knew that she was ready too.

"I don't know how to thank you

enough," she said to her godmother.

"Thank me by being back by midnight!"

Midnight is hours from now. Why

does she keep harping on about midnight? Cinderella wondered. I'll probably want to leave a long time before that.

"Midnight, or there's going to be a very serious consequence!" her fairy godmother shouted, running alongside the carriage as it clip-clopped away.

"Definitely by midnight," Cinderella called back.

From inside the carriage Cinderella noticed that she lit up the landscape around her. If she smiled, everyone on the street looked happy. If she frowned, so did they.

As the carriage slowed to a stop outside the palace gates, one of the lizards—now a coachman—offered his arm to steady Cinderella down the carriage steps.

chapter 6

The massive palace door groaned open, and Cinderella glimpsed a world as orderly and well mannered as a clock. Impeccably dressed couples danced tidy minuets on elaborately patterned floors.

But with Cinderella's entrance into the ballroom, everything stopped. The threads of conversations snapped, violin strings stopped vibrating, and even loud colors fell silent. Not a medal or a monocle glistened, not an ostrich feather wavered.

"I say, darling, who is that lovely?"

"Let me look through my opera glasses, Bubsy.

Oh, look at that. It *is* a princess,

you can *always* spot them."

There was a gasp as anyone standing near a column leaned against it for strength.

Half the guests whispered, "Who is that?"

The other half shook their heads and gestured that they didn't know.

Above the gold chandeliers, the opulent hors d'oeuvres, the fringed curtains, and the potted palms stood the king and queen, looking down on it all. Up there in that exalted world of cloud-painted ceilings and operatic arias, their crowns had begun to weigh heavily on their heads. You could see it in the lopsided way they smiled at each other.

Spellbound, the impeccably dressed
couples watched as the prince walked

all the way across the giant room

to ask Cinderella with an eloquent ges-
ture if she would care to dance.

"I'd be delighted, Your Highness."

Where had she learned to speak as
royally as that? Cinderella wondered.

And so Cinderella and the prince
danced as though they had always
known each other. People's necks

lengthened, their jokes became funnier, and the tuba player improvised a melodious solo. The laughter, clinking of glasses, straightening of bow ties, and beckoning of waiters became bigger, livelier, and louder.

The couple danced and danced, circumventing Doric columns, dodging

Thank goodness she doesn't know that my mother made me take dance classes!

waiters with silver trays. It was only when they stopped dancing that things got awkward.

"Let's get some air," said the prince.

"All right," replied Cinderella.

They stepped out onto the balcony and into the moonlight. She looked marvelous, he told her. Well, his dancing was sublime, she told him.

Thank goodness he doesn't know I got a total makeover from my fairy godmother!

With nothing left to say, they returned to the ballroom and let the saxophones and violins speak for them.

For the rest of the evening, the music carried them wherever it wanted. They never did get around to exchanging names and phone numbers.

Thanks to years of dance instruction, the prince expertly fox-trotted Cinderella over to a red-carpeted part of the room, cordoned off by a velvet rope. A royal mountain of filet mignon and cubes of quivering Jell-O in jewel-like colors awaited. A general was carving some steak. A royal waiter balanced glasses of champagne on a silver tray. Two cousins of the prince helped themselves from dessert tables piled high with whipped cream, studded with imperial berries, and flecked with colored sprinkles.

"All my favorite foods," the prince explained, loudly enough to be heard over the music, as they helped themselves to a little bit of everything.

"Why no yellow sprinkles?" Cinderella mouthed back.

"I don't like those as much, so they take them out," said the prince.

"Oh," Cinderella replied, and her mouth stayed in a circle.

chapter 7

When Cinderella looked over her shoulder to see what all the commotion was about, she was surprised to see her two stepsisters at the center of it all. Their hair had stayed up nicely, she noticed with satisfaction. The two of them were loudly lambasting a man in tights who was guarding the velvet rope.

"It isn't exactly fair. . . ."

"The food looks better in there, and it's carpeted. . . ."

"I am so very sorry," the man in tights told them stiffly. "This section is strictly for the cream of the crop, their close friends, and hangers-on."

"Are you calling us hoi polloi?"

"Suggesting we are riffraff?"

"*Mesdemoiselles*, you must understand I am here to follow the wishes of the king and queen."

It didn't seem fair to Cinderella either. Why should she be on one side while her own stepsisters were stuck on the other? Without thinking, she scooped up two chocolates wrapped in gold and handed them to her stepsisters as consolation. The prince, glancing up from his filet mignon, was touched by Cinderella's generosity.

Suddenly, Cinderella felt a pang of worry. Might the sight of their step-sister lolling about in the red-carpeted zone instead of doing laundry back home bring on a fresh round of indigna-tion? She froze momentar-ily at the thought. But it was obvious by the way the girls blushed and curtsied that they did not rec-ognize her.

Her head was in the clouds, and she could tell the prince's was too. She had almost forgotten the other world where she used to live. None of that seemed real anymore. Then she heard the clock begin to chime and looked to see what time it was.

⸻⬥⸻

"Yikes!" Cinderella gasped, her royal syntax falling away.

The prince was too busy helping a blob of emerald green Jell-O onto a spoon to notice her dashing out. Neither did anyone else as they moonwalked and lollygagged across the floor.

As Cinderella ran across the ballroom, her left shoe fell off.

By the massive door she felt herself grow lighter and swifter. Her gown had vanished, and she was back in her old clothes again. Outside, she noticed a rat lumbering off into the shadows and several smaller creatures scuttling away. A solitary pumpkin sat by the side of the road. Cinderella took off the remaining shoe, tucked it into her pocket, and ran barefoot all the way home.

"I guess I got my consequence," she thought.

Cinderella went straight up to her room. Turning on the little lamp by her bed, she began to try to make sense of what had happened.

Dear Mama,

If you were still here I might not want to talk to you about this, because you would ~~probably~~ laugh and maybe tell all your friends. But, I guess, well, here goes: I think I might really be in love. I mean for real. That's the good part. The strange part is that it is with this prince, who I don't even know (apart from what his favorite foods are). I can tell he loves me back, which

should also be a good part. But
he thinks I am someone else
who I'm really not, which is just
terrible. I'll explain that in a minute.
I guess I'll never even see him again,

which is ~~absolutely~~ the
part I can't believe.
   I still feel airborne.
This is going to make
doing chores again feel like
a real thud. ~~But~~ Okay,
now let me back up
a bit....

Cinderella wrote several pages ex-
plaining in great detail how her fairy
godmother had appeared out of
nowhere and turned useless stuff

around the house into everything she had needed to go to the ball. When she was done she could imagine the look on her mother's face, so she added,

p.s. Listen, I know it's asking a lot to expect you to believe all any of what I've written here. Just think about the fact that you are reading this letter — that's pretty strange too. So you see, you never know.

Underneath she drew a funny picture of a person looking surprised, with her mouth open and her hair standing on end.

chapter 8

Meanwhile, back at the ball, one of the prince's servants brought him the little shoe left on the floor. The mystery girl had gone

without

even saying

goodbye!

Mournfully carrying the shoe on a small velvet pillow, he asked the servants who stood near the doors if any of them had seen a lady with just one shoe leaving in a bit of a hurry.

None of them had.

The prince felt happy and sad at the same time—happy to have found the girl of his dreams, sad to have lost her. His stomach lurched as if he were on a roller coaster. The mystery girl was so gloriously different from his mother, he thought, as he watched the queen waddle off to her bedchamber. His mother was a stickler for introductions; she would *never* go without saying goodbye. He laughed out loud at the idea of his mother leaving a shoe behind.

The prince took a quick inventory. He was happier than he had ever been. He was sadder than he had ever been. Nobody had ever ditched him or enchanted him like this.

He could never marry anyone else. He would like to marry her. All of which meant he needed urgently to find her. Right away, whatever her name was.

⚫

While the prince was pining for her, Cinderella heard voices outside her

window and pretended to be fast asleep. Stomping loudly up to her room, her stepsisters had a lot to say. "You were such an idiot not to come," began the elder.

"You should kick yourself!" suggested the younger.

Cinderella tried to look suitably distressed. Next her stepsisters proudly displayed the chocolates—the ones she herself had given them earlier.

"Look, but don't touch!" said the elder.

"Did someone *give* them to you?" asked Cinderella slowly, trying to sound curious.

"Not just *someone!*" scoffed the elder.

"How can we even explain it to her?" lamented the younger sister.

"Girls!"

Their mother shouted up the stairway.

"Get to bed, girls.

You two need your

beauty sleep and

Cinderella has a
lot of work to do in
the morning."

chapter 9

He needed to find the mysterious girl. By the next morning the prince had begun to pace. What else could he do besides walk around in circles? His very life hung in the balance, he thought. It was all so desperately glorious and gloriously desperate.

It shocked the prince to see how alone he was. His parents, who until recently had seemed such reasonable creatures, wanted to know why the whole business couldn't be discussed over dinner after a civilized game of golf.

"Golf—during a national crisis?" The prince could hardly believe his ears.

It had begun to occur to the prince that his parents were a lot less wise and witty than he had once thought. Their jokes, for example, were not really all that funny. People laughed so loudly because they were the king and queen. Now the awful knowledge that his parents were actually a couple of complete imbeciles crashed down on the prince's head. As he watched them lumber off with their golf clubs, it was suddenly obvious: he would have to handle this all by himself.

The prince summoned the royal advisors.

"The person who fits this shoe will be my wife," he told them, holding up the dainty shoe on a velvet pillow.

"All sorts of other people might fit that particular shoe, Your Highness. . . ."

"A boy, and not a girl, could easily . . ."

"Judging from the size of it, the person might still be in elementary school . . ."

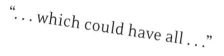

". . . which could have all . . ."

". . . sorts of legal ramifications."

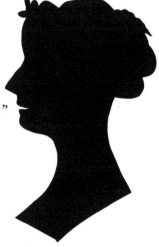

The prince was exasperated by their ridiculous drivel.

"I guess I'll just have to look for her by myself," he declared.

The prince asked two servants to have his finest horse saddled. He put on a full suit of armor and wielded a mighty sword. A little flag would add a nice touch, he decided. The prince himself carefully bore the tiny shoe on the small velvet cushion. The servants came along to help with map reading, bugle blowing, and knocking on doors.

Because Cinderella had seemed so at home fox-trotting past portraits of his

titled ancestors, the prince felt sure she was well-to-do.

"She must live up one of these long driveways, or perhaps in a gated community," the prince told his servants as they started on their quest.

Word of the princely expedition had spread, and girls from hoity-toity families thrust their feet delicately out of windows to save His Highness the mortification of speaking with their own particular mothers and fathers.

Alas, every female foot in the high-end neighborhoods proved too big for the tiny shoe. Now the prince pictured a lonely life ahead of

him—devoted to writing love poetry with a quill pen.

"Such a brief moment of happiness," he despaired, "and now an eternity of sorrow."

In these moods the prince could be a royal pain. So as they knocked on doors of the non-hoity-toity, his servants did their best to humor him.

"Perhaps it is she, and not her family, who is noble," the first suggested.

The thought had never occurred to the prince, and he knew immediately that his servant was right.

"You should be proud of this brave undertaking whatever the outcome," said the other, and the prince realized he was. Very proud. These two short men were wiser than all his royal advisors and his parents put together. He had been so right to leave home and head out like this on his own . . . almost.

No one else in his family had done anything half this hard, or risky, or romantic, he thought. He pictured how good he must look wearing his armor, glinting in the sunlight, with the flag fluttering in the breeze. If he couldn't respect his parents anymore, at least he could look up to himself. The thought cheered him.

Startled by a loud rap on the door, followed by a noisy bugle salute, Cinderella's stepmother strode angrily forward.

"Who is it now?" she shouted. She had already forgotten what came next on the list of chores she was writing out for Cinderella.

She opened the door a crack, and the sight of the prince at the bottom of the garden path, resplendent in a full suit of armor, turned her scowl into a fawning smile.

"His Royal Highness the prince asks that all unmarried ladies in this house try on this particular shoe," announced one of the servants, waving an impossibly small ivory and gold shoe on a little velvet pillow.

actual size

"It is his personal wish," added the other servant, importantly.

The two stepsisters skidded to a stop in the front hallway. They had heard about the prince's search for a wife based on her shoe size.

"It fits!"

shouted the elder as she stuffed her foot into the teensy shoe, her heel poking way out in the back.

The prince's servant could see she was lying, so he motioned to her sister to try on the shoe. Her feet were even bigger, so the second sister suggested,

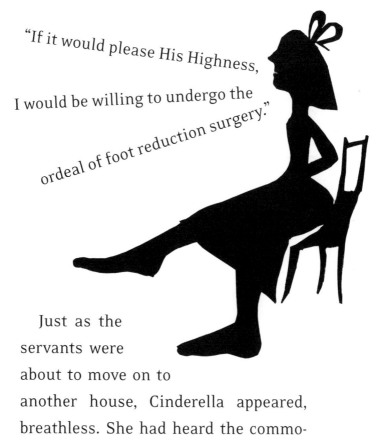

"If it would please His Highness, I would be willing to undergo the ordeal of foot reduction surgery."

Just as the servants were about to move on to another house, Cinderella appeared, breathless. She had heard the commotion and dashed all the way down from

her room in the attic to see if there was
something she could do to help.

Smiling at the lost ivory and gold shoe as if at an old friend, she slipped it on. Then she pulled its mate out of her pocket and put that shoe on her other foot.

At the end of the garden path, the prince was beside himself with joy. He had found her at last!

As quickly as he could in a full suit of armor, the prince dismounted his horse and dashed up the pathway. It touched him to see that, like

him, his beloved was surrounded by idiotic family members. The two of them had so much in common, the prince thought, fighting back the tears.

As he drew near, the prince saw that the girl he had danced with looked even more adorable in her regular clothes. He loved her more now—even though he wouldn't have thought that was possible. He felt so awkward encased in armor. He wished it weren't so hard to move. . . . He wished . . . he knew her name.

Shyly, the prince whispered to one of his servants to inquire what the girl's name might be.

"Cinderella," Cinderella said happily, hearing the question.

At that the prince nervously dropped to one knee. His armor scraped noisily

into its new position and made a clank-
ing noise.

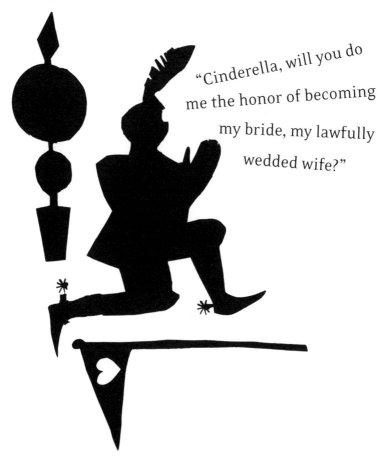

"Cinderella, will you do
me the honor of becoming
my bride, my lawfully
wedded wife?"

His fate was in her hands now.

As Cinderella's jaw dropped in amazement, a whole ripple of events took place. First her fairy godmother appeared out of nowhere. An expert wave of her wand turned Cinderella back into the dazzling beauty of the night before.

Then her stepsisters, who could see that it was their own Cinderella who

had danced with the prince, began to sob.

"Please, please forgive us!
We didn't know it was you!"

"We had no idea!"

Before she could even consider the royal proposal, Cinderella knew she had to get the noise to stop. She begged her stepsisters to quit boohooing. She helped them wipe the mascara off their cheeks.

Then Cinderella turned her attention to the prince. He looked terrible. It had been a full minute since he had asked for her hand in marriage and he was forgetting to breathe.

"Hmmmmmm," Cinderella said. Should she marry the prince? She just wasn't sure. She didn't really even *know* the guy, apart from, well, his favorite foods. He certainly was a good dancer . . . but then again. . . . Cinderella's heart beat loudly in her chest.

chapter 10

At last the answer came to her. "Yes," said Cinderella, smiling radiantly.

"Yes!" she said again.

The prince hugged her and told her how overjoyed he was. Then he thanked the two servants who had accompanied him on his royal quest. Then he said he would never take anything for granted for the rest of his life. Then the fairy

godmother and the stepsisters and
Cinderella's father and even
her stepmother needed to wipe
their faces with handkerchiefs

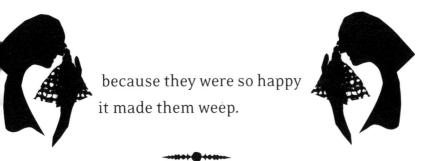

because they were so happy
it made them weep.

Usually this is when the curtain flops
down with the words

*Happily
Ever
After.*

But there is more, of course, and I don't
see why you shouldn't hear it.

As days became weeks, and weeks became months, Cinderella and the prince discovered that they were actually as different as a tree and a lake. It was hard sometimes, but it opened up a big landscape of possibilities for both of them. As the love between them grew, they began to trust themselves, even the dark scary places.

Dear Mama,

So much has happened with the peace treaties and the trade agreements lately, I hardly know where to begin.

The most important thing, though, is I think the prince loves me just the way I am even when I make mistakes.

Thank you, Mama, for everything always.

Your Cupcake

The prince was no longer afraid of his own emotions; in fact, he wallowed in them. As king now, he sang songs—songs about his soppiest, saddest, most heartfelt feelings. They were songs that made people bring out their handkerchiefs to dab their tears away.

Cinderella was no longer a pushover. Her toughness as a diplomat brought a period of peace. With no wars, her husband's suit of armor was no longer needed, and it became a curious object that people stared at in a glass case in a museum.

"We want wildness!" Queen Cinderella told her astonished subjects in her new strong voice. "The best rooms in the kingdom will become places where birds can heal their broken wings and tired bats can rest." She and the king had already moved out of the palace into more modest accommodations.

"But your stepmother and I are very old now," Queen Cinderella's father begged.

"Oh, all right, you may stay on in that big house, provided you clean up after the pigs."

Her stepmother thanked Queen Cinderella for her generosity and swore she would sweep and mop night and day.

Queen Cinderella's stepsisters begged to be allowed to stay on as well. They desperately needed all that closet space for their fancy clothes, they explained.

"Desperately."

"Horribly."

"Not a chance," the queen's messenger told them. "The animals are moving in tomorrow."

So you see, nowadays, Queen Cinderella isn't afraid of anyone or anything. Nobody is her boss.

And

that

really

is

The
End

YOU ALREADY KNEW THIS STORY

NO MATTER WHERE IN THE WORLD YOU GREW UP OR WHEN YOU LIVED.

IN CHINA THE FAIRY GODMOTHER IS A DEAD FISH WHICH USED TO BE HER PET.

HER MOM DOESN'T DIE IN INDIA. INSTEAD SHE GETS TURNED INTO A GOAT. IN DENMARK MOM IS STUCK BEING A COW.

SHE GOT TOO CLOSE TO THE FIRE, THE ALGONQUINS SAY, WHICH IS WHY HER HAIR CAUGHT ON FIRE AND HER FACE GOT ALL SCARRED LIKE THAT.

GERMANS SAY THINGS END BADLY FOR THE STEPSISTERS: THEY GET THEIR EYES PECKED OUT BY BIRDS.

IN ZIMBABWE IT'S A MAGIC SNAKE THAT HELPS HER. SOMETIMES THERE IS NO BALL. A HAWK JUST TAKES ONE SHOE DIRECTLY TO THE PRINCE.

about the author

As if everyone doesn't already know,
Barbara Ensor has written for *New York
Magazine, Entertainment Weekly,
Family Life*, the *Village Voice*, and
numerous other publications and Web sites.
Her illustrations have appeared in the *New
York Times, Harper's Magazine, Self,* and
Graphis, among others.

She grew up mostly in London. Her first job
after graduating from Brown University was
as a traveling puppeteer—which
occasionally required her to walk on stilts.
Barbara Ensor is the mother of two children
and lives a fairy-tale life in
Brooklyn, New York.